# SPIDER
# AND THE
# SKY GOD

To my grandparents,
Quinnie and Annie Newton.
With love,
DMC

*Library of Congress Cataloging-in-Publication Data*

Chocolate, Deborah M. Newton.
   Spider and the Sky God: an Akan legend / retold by Deborah M.
Newton Chocolate; illustrated by Dave Albers.
      p.     cm. (Legends of the world)
   Summary: Ananse the Spider uses trickery to capture the four
prizes demanded by the Sky God in payment for his stories.
   ISBN 0-8167-2811-9 (lib. bdg.)      ISBN 0-8167-2812-7 (pbk.)
   1. Anansi (Legendary character)—Legends.  [1. Anansi (Legendary
character)  2. Folklore—Ghana.]  I. Albers, Dave, 1961-     ill.
II. Title.  III. Series.
PZ8.1.C4517 Sp  1993
398.24′52544—dc20                                                    92-13277

# SPIDER
## AND THE SKY GOD
### AN AKAN LEGEND

**RETOLD BY DEBORAH M. NEWTON CHOCOLATE    ILLUSTRATED BY DAVE ALBERS**

TROLL ASSOCIATES

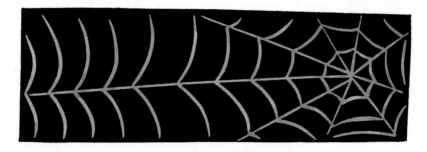

Long ago in Africa, long before there were stories on earth, there lived a Spider named Ananse. Ananse spun the most beautiful spider webs in all his village. But his secret wish was to spin stories and tales as splendid as his webs. Ananse knew that all the stories belonged to the Sky God.

So, one day, Ananse threw his silk web up, up, up to the sky. When he reached the court of the great Sky God, Ananse bowed low to the ground.

"O, God of All Things," he said. "I wish to know, what is the price of your stories?"

Seated before the elders, Sky God laughed. "Greater ones than you have come to buy my stories, Kwaku Ananse."

Sky God looked at the Spider's spindly legs and choked through his laughter. "Someone so tiny, so tiny as you could never pay the price!"

"I shall pay whatever price you ask," insisted the Spider.

So Sky God answered Ananse. "My stories cannot be bought, except that you bring me these four things: Onini—the Python, Mmoboro—the buzzing Hornets, Osebo—the Leopard, and Mmoatia—the Fairy."

"I will bring you all of these things," Ananse promised boldly.

So Ananse the Spider threw his silk web down, down, down and scrambled back to earth. Aso, his wife, was cooking plantain and yam mash in their hut. He told her all about Sky God and what he must do to buy his stories.

As they sat down to eat, he asked, "What is to be done that we may capture Onini the Python?"

Aso answered, "Cut a branch from a palm tree. Also cut some vine-creeper. Then take them to the river where Onini the Python lives."

Ananse headed for the river. As he walked along, the Spider talked out loud. He was all by himself, but he pretended that Aso his wife was walking beside him.

"But it *is* longer than Onini," he said.

"It *is not* as long as Onini!"

"Tell the truth. It is longer, longer, very much longer than Onini."

Then Ananse said, "There is Brother Python lying near the river. Let us ask him ourselves."

Having overheard this imaginary argument, the Python inquired, "What is all this talk of Onini about?"

"It is I, Ananse the Spider, and my wife Aso, who is arguing with me that this palm branch is longer than you. I say that it is not true."

Onini the Python thought for a moment and then said, "Come, measure me with the palm branch. Then we will see which of you is right."

Ananse laid the palm branch down beside the Python's long body. "You must stretch yourself," said Ananse. Python did as he was told. Then the Spider took the vine and quickly wound it around Python and the palm branch.

*Thwitt! Thwitt! Thwitt!* was the sound of the tying, till Ananse came to Python's head. Now certain that Onini could not escape, the Spider stopped tying and shouted, "Ho! I shall take you up to Sky God and receive his tales in exchange!"

Ananse was so pleased with himself that on the way home he spun the most beautiful web.

When Ananse reached home, he told Aso what had happened, adding, "Now there are the Hornets to catch."

His wife said, "Look for a calabash bowl, and fill it up with water. Then go to the forest."

The Spider did as she suggested, carrying the calabash into the forest. Soon he heard the sound of Mmoboro the buzzing Hornets, hanging in the still air. He climbed a nearby tree and sprinkled water on them. The rest of the water he poured over himself. Then he covered his head with a plantain leaf.

Ananse spoke to the Hornets. "The rains have come,
my brothers. Perhaps, you had better shelter yourselves in
this calabash bowl of mine, so the rains will not drown
you. Can't you see that I cover myself with this plantain
leaf to keep dry?"

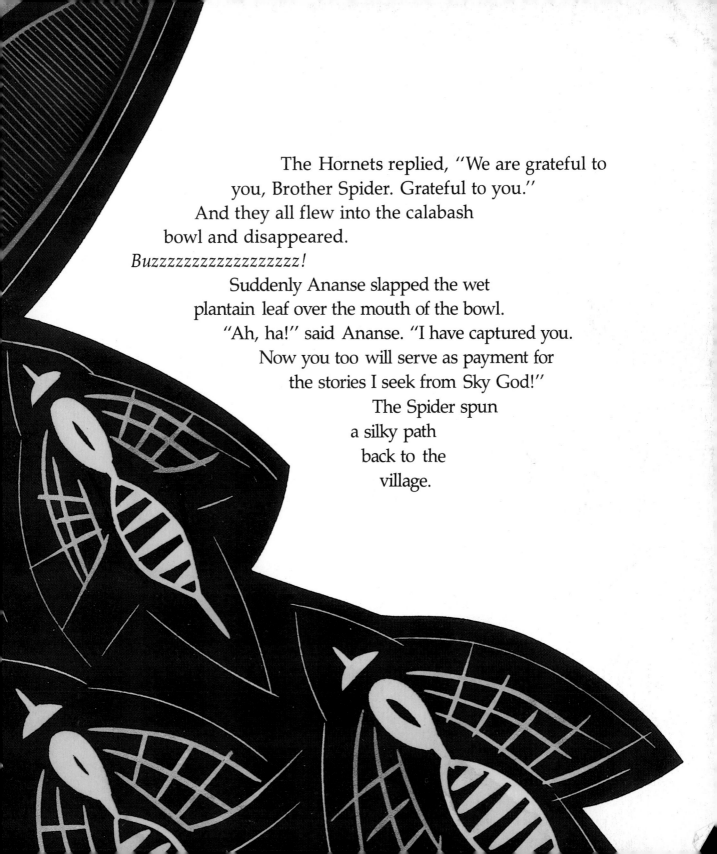

The Hornets replied, "We are grateful to
you, Brother Spider. Grateful to you."
And they all flew into the calabash
bowl and disappeared.
*Buzzzzzzzzzzzzzzzzz!*
Suddenly Ananse slapped the wet
plantain leaf over the mouth of the bowl.
"Ah, ha!" said Ananse. "I have captured you.
Now you too will serve as payment for
the stories I seek from Sky God!"
The Spider spun
a silky path
back to the
village.

"Now there is Osebo the Leopard to catch," Ananse said to his wife.

Aso told him, "You must dig a deep hole."

So the Spider set off in search of Leopard's tracks. Once he found them, he dug a deep hole in the path. He covered the hole with branches and returned to the village. Early the next morning, Ananse went back to the forest.

He found the Leopard lying at the bottom of the pit and called out to him, "Oh, Brother Leopard, I have warned you not to drink of the fruit of the palm tree. Now look at you. You have fallen into this pit. If I were to get you out, surely tomorrow you would try to eat me and my children."

The Leopard replied, "Oh no, Brother. I could never do anything as bad as that."

"But still, I am afraid you would," the Spider insisted.

"Ananse," begged the Leopard, "if you help me get out, I will never catch you or your children, nor any of your cousins."

Ananse cut two bamboo sticks from a nearby grove. He stuck one bamboo stick into one wall of the pit. Then he pushed the other stick into the wall opposite and said to Leopard, "Place one paw here and the other there." Leopard did as Ananse instructed.

Out of sight of Leopard was a cage near the top edge of the pit. As Leopard climbed up, Ananse lifted the door of the cage, then let it slap down. *Thump!* Leopard was trapped in the cage.

"Foolish, foolish Leopard! Now I will trade you for the stories of Sky God."

Ananse was very pleased with himself. Along the path, a beautiful spider web followed Ananse to his hut.

When Ananse reached the village, he carved a flat-faced wooden doll, an Akua's child, from an odum tree. He tapped some sticky fluid from a gum tree and painted the doll's face and body with it. Then he pounded eto from mashed yams. He put some eto in the doll's hand. He pounded more yams and put them in a brass pot. After tying a string around the doll's waist, he took the doll and placed it at the foot of the odum tree, the place where Fairies came to play.

Along came Mmoatia the Fairy. Mmoatia asked the doll, "Akua, may I eat some of your mash?"

Ananse jerked the string, and the doll nodded her head and did a little dance.

"She says I may eat some."

When the Fairy finished eating, she thanked the doll, but this time the doll did not answer. "Perhaps she is asleep. I will open her eyes with my hand."

When Mmoatia tried to open the doll's eyes, her hand stuck there in the gum. "My hand is stuck!" she cried. "I will take my other hand and try again."

Now both hands were stuck fast. She pushed against the doll with her foot, and it, too, was stuck.

Suddenly Ananse jumped out from behind the tree. "Now I have you!" he shouted. "I shall take you to Sky God, and he will give me his tales."

And the Spider went back to the village with the Fairy in his spider web.

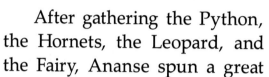 After gathering the Python, the Hornets, the Leopard, and the Fairy, Ananse spun a great web around his catch. He threw his silk web up, up, up to the sky. When Ananse reached the court of the great Sky God, he bowed low to the ground.

"O God of All Things, here are Onini the Python, Mmoboro the Hornets, Osebo the Leopard, and Mmoatia the Fairy. All are payment for your stories."

Then Sky God called his court of elders. He put the matter before them. "Great kings have come and gone, unable to pay the price for my stories. But here before us is Kwaku Ananse. He has given me Onini the Python, Mmoboro the Hornets, Osebo the Leopard, and Mmoatia the Fairy. We must sing praise to Kwaku Ananse."

"*Eeee!*" shouted the elders.

"Kwaku Ananse," said the Sky God, "from now on and forever, I give my stories to you. *Kose! Kose! Kose!* Bless you! Bless you! Bless you! No more shall they be known as stories of Sky God, but we shall call them Spider Stories."

And so it came to be that Ananse traveled
from town to town, spinning his splendid
Spider tales. Sometimes he told them with
mime and music. But always the stories
lived on in the listeners' memories.

Ananse the Spider is the hero of stories told by the Akan people of West Africa. The Akan include several tribes in the southwest part of the country of Ghana. *Spider and the Sky God* is a legend all about storytelling. It is an example of a "why" story, or a story that tells of how something came to be.

Ananse is a tricky fellow—greedy and cunning, but very likeable. Through his cleverness, Ananse is able to overpower many larger animals. Around the world, some of the most popular stories are about the trickster. In America's Southwest, the trickster is a coyote. In the Pacific Northwest, he is a raven. Brer Rabbit is also a trickster, just like Ananse. Trickster stories are marked by a sharp sense of humor that exposes human nature.

Storytelling was very important to the Akan, even before they had written language. It taught their children valuable lessons about life. The Akan storyteller, often a woman, would say prayers before telling her stories. Many of the stories would tell about the relationship between people and God.

African storytelling involves everyone; listeners chant and sing choruses that become part of the storyteller's tale and often answer her questions. As the story builds, the storyteller even acts out the characters' roles while the audience joins in.

The stories of Ananse traveled from Africa to the New World with the slaves. In the American South, they are known as "Aunt Nancy" stories. In the Caribbean, they have survived as "Anancy" stories. But in his African homeland, they are still called "Spider Stories."